The Wrong Door

Written by Brandon Robshaw

Illustrated by Elisa Rocchi

Collins

Chapter 1

Molly had no idea what lay in store as she stood
outside the door of the Holiday Club. She could hear
a roomful of children she didn't know. For a moment,
she felt like running away, but then she'd have nowhere
to go all day, she'd get in trouble and still have to come
back tomorrow.

She tapped softly on the door. It opened immediately.

"Good morning!" A smiling woman ushered Molly in.

"Welcome to the Holiday Club! My name's Gloria. And you are …?"

"Molly," said Molly, in a whisper.

"What was that? Holly?"

"No, Molly," said Molly, a tiny bit louder.

"Oh, Polly, is it?"

"No, it's *Molly*!" said Molly in her loudest voice. A hush fell and all the children turned round to look at her. Somebody giggled.

"Oh, yes. Molly Atkins," said Gloria, ticking her name off on a list. "Take a seat. There's squash and biscuits, help yourself."

There were three other children at Molly's table: two girls and a boy. They all smiled at her.

"Hi!" said one of the girls. "I'm Rani."

"I'm Molly."

"Yeah, we heard!" said the other girl, and everybody laughed. Were they laughing *with* her? Or *at* her?

Molly felt her face going red. She reached out for
the orange squash jug but knocked it over. The others
jumped back, and the boy said, "That nearly *got* me!"

There were songs, games, painting ... The children from her table seemed nice. Shirelle was funny, cracking jokes all the time. Blake was loud and enthusiastic about everything, singing songs at the top of his voice. And Rani was very friendly, asking Molly questions, trying to start a conversation.

But Molly felt too shy. She sat in the corner, saying and doing as little as possible. Her friends at school would have been surprised to see how quiet she was. When Molly was with people she knew well, she hardly stopped talking. But with strangers ... well, that was different.

She wished the day would end. But even when today ended, she'd have to come back again tomorrow.

If only her dad had let her go to work with him!
Or her mum. But they had both said there would be
nothing for her to do there.

"It'll be much more fun at the Holiday Club!" her dad
had said.

And it might have been, if her friends from school
were here too. But they were all away on holiday with
their families.

At lunchtime, Molly decided to escape. Gloria and the helpers were busy setting out sandwiches and pizza. No one would notice if she sidled out and went for a wander. A *wander*. Molly liked that word. It made her think of space, freedom and exploration.

She quietly wandered out through the door and into a corridor.

Chapter 2

The Holiday Club was in Buston Civic Centre – a vast building that housed the Town Hall, a library, a leisure centre, a café and lots of meeting rooms.

At first, Molly enjoyed exploring. There were colourful abstract paintings on the walls. There was a sculpture of a dolphin rising out of the sea. She came to a hall with a fountain. There were corridors leading off it that led to stairs and more corridors, which went into more rooms. The place was like a maze.

Molly began to feel worried. Would she be able to find her way back to the Holiday Club? She wished she had left a trail of breadcrumbs behind her like Hansel and Gretel.

She tried to retrace her steps. There was a door at the end of a corridor that looked identical to the one she had come out of.

She pushed it open and found herself in a big gleaming kitchen. A woman in a chef's hat turned round from the stove.

"Hello there! You must be Milly! You're early!"

"Er ..." Not knowing what to say, Molly smiled politely.

The woman grinned back. "Well, you're here – that's the main thing. I'm Rowena. You must be a phenomenal cook."

"Oh, must I?"

"Well, you don't win Junior Baker of the Year unless you're something pretty special! Your prize is a day in the kitchen with me – and you're going to help prepare the seven-course banquet for the Awards Ceremony! Here, put these on." Rowena threw a stripy blue-and-white apron and a chef's hat at her.

Molly should have confessed that she wasn't Junior Baker of the Year, couldn't cook anything apart from toast and instant noodles, and had simply come through the wrong door. But Rowena seemed so nice and friendly. And maybe it would be fun to try cooking, with no other children watching.

"How about some cake decoration?"

That sounded all right, Molly thought. An impressively large sponge cake stood on the worktop. Beside it were bowls of different coloured icing. Rowena handed her a piping bag – a conical plastic bag with a nozzle sticking out of the bottom.

"Just use your imagination – be as artistic as you like!"

"Er, right," said Molly. Gingerly, she spooned white icing into the bag. Some of it fell down the front of the apron, but some ended up in the piping bag. Rowena smiled at her encouragingly.

"I won't watch. I don't want to put you off. Surprise me!"

Molly looked at the cake. What could she decorate it with? A cat? Everyone likes cats.

Molly began to draw a big, fat cat's body. But the piping bag was hard to control. The icing came out in a splurge. She refilled the bag, with green icing this time, and drew a rather wonky head. In pink icing, she gave it big sweeping whiskers that looked like tentacles. And then in blue icing, she supplied two little ears and two big eyes. Splotches of coloured icing surrounded the cat like a fireworks display.

"Finished?" said Rowena. She came and looked at Molly's handiwork. A puzzled look came over her face. "Have you ever decorated a cake before?"

"No," said Molly in a small voice.

"Then what ...?"

18

"I'm not the Junior Baker of the Year!" said Molly, all in a rush. "I'm in the Holiday Club. I came through the wrong door."

Rowena looked at Molly, then at the cake, then back at Molly.

Then she burst out laughing.

Chapter 3

Molly found herself back in the maze-like corridors of the Civic Centre. She had to find her way back to the Holiday Club. They would surely have missed her by now.

Her heart leapt in recognition as she came to the space where the fountain was playing. But there were four corridors leading off it. Well, the one she had just come along could be ruled out. The middle one *looked* right. She hoped there would be some pizza left ...

As she approached a door, she heard a piano. Molly liked singing. Maybe it would be a fun afternoon.

She pushed open the door. A young man was sitting at a black, glossy grand piano, idly playing chords. He turned from the keyboard and smiled at Molly.

"Well, hello! Come for the rehearsal?"

"Rehearsal?"

"I know you must know it by heart, but a run-through won't hurt."

"I don't ..." Molly stood twisting her hands together like a pair of wrestling octopuses. She wanted to say she had come through the wrong door. Again. But she felt tongue-tied. "I'm not ..."

Why not? she suddenly thought. *After all, I had a go at decorating the cake? And even though I messed it up, nothing terrible happened ...*

Molly sat at the keyboard.

The pianist smiled encouragingly. "Let's hear what you can do!"

Molly had never learnt to play the piano. But she did know one tune: *Chopsticks*. You start by playing two keys next to each other, then gradually widening the distance between the notes until they are an octave apart, and then come back together again. You only need two fingers, but it sounded, Molly thought, quite impressive.

But the pianist clearly didn't agree. When Molly finished, he was frowning in a puzzled manner.

"That's not Schubert's *Fantasia in F Minor*, is it?"

Molly shook her head.

"Are you not the talented young pianist Maria von Langersnacken, who is scheduled to play a duet with me at the Buston Young Person of the Year Award this afternoon?"

Molly shook her head. "I just came in the wrong door."

A smile spread over the pianist's face. "I'm so sorry! You must have thought I was crazy!"

As Molly went out, she heard him start to play *Chopsticks*. He was laughing.

Chapter 4

The fountain tinkled merrily. Molly looked at the two corridors she hadn't tried yet. The one on the right looked somehow more inviting. Yes, that had to be the one.

She realised she had made another miscalculation when she walked out on to a stage at the front of a huge hall with lots of tables occupied by women in long dresses and men in suits. Above the stage hung a massive banner which said, "BUSTON YOUNG PERSON OF THE YEAR AWARDS".

Three children of about Molly's age were sitting on chairs on the stage. So was the Lord Mayor of Buston in his robes and gold chain. And so was an elegant woman in a blue suit wearing a badge that read "Liza Dreiser: Organiser".

Liza Dreiser came towards Molly. "Thank goodness you're here at last! Now we can begin. Lovely choice of shirt, by the way!"

Molly looked at her T-shirt. It had a picture of a donkey in a straw hat chewing a carrot. She couldn't see anything special about it.

Molly was ushered to the one remaining empty seat. She couldn't get off the stage now without attracting a lot of attention.

Liza Dreiser moved to the front of the platform and a hush fell over the hall.

"Ladies and gentlemen, we are here to celebrate the achievements of four extraordinary children: animal-lover Peter Pilgrim, budding artist Nicola Johnson, young scientist Kevin Nevin, and Jessica Brooke, whose moving articles on donkey sanctuaries have appeared in the *Buston Recorder*. And later, we will be treated to a piano recital by Maria von Langersnacken, the Buston Young Musician of the Year, and we will feast on a banquet prepared by Milly Grimshaw, the Buston Junior Baker of the Year!"

Applause filled the hall.

"These remarkable children will all receive awards this afternoon. But in addition, there will be an *overall* award for the Buston Young Person of the Year, to be judged by the mayor. To help the mayor decide, each of the young people will give a short speech explaining their achievement. So without further ado, I give you ... Peter Pilgrim!"

Peter gave a long and boring account of how he'd saved a dog from drowning in the canal.

Then Nicola took the stage and gave a rather self-admiring speech about the artistic influences that had enabled her to win a painting competition.

Then Kevin gave an incomprehensible account full of scientific words about how to grow super-length cucumbers.

Molly was bored by the speeches but also wished they would go on for longer. What was she going to say about donkeys?

All too soon, Liza Dreiser beckoned her to the front of the platform. And suddenly Molly thought, *How hard can it be? I've already had a go at decorating a cake and playing the piano today. OK, so I messed up both times, but nothing terrible happened ...*

"Ladies and gentlemen ..."
(*Not a bad start*, thought Molly.)
"I wrote those articles about
donkey sanctuaries because ..."
(*Still OK, but now what?*)
"... Because donkeys are very
nice animals. Nice animals with
long, velvety noses. Like this one
on my T-shirt. Isn't it beautiful?"

Molly spotted the pianist in
the front next to a girl she guessed
was Maria, and near him sat
Rowena the chef and a girl who
must be Milly. Both professionals
smiled at Molly. Her confidence
began to increase.

"They have long ears, donkeys do.
Of course, other animals have long
ears as well. Such as rabbits. But then,
rabbits are also nice animals.
Donkeys eat carrots. Just like
the one on my T-shirt."

Laughter rippled around the hall.

They like it! thought Molly. Emboldened, she pressed on. "And come to think of it, rabbits eat carrots too. So ... maybe donkeys and rabbits are related. With their long ears and shared love of carrots."

More laughter. The audience certainly seemed to be appreciating Molly's speech more than the others.

"Who knows? But it's good that they have sanctuaries. Donkeys, I mean. But then, maybe rabbits should have sanctuaries, too. Maybe ..."

She paused. A rather neat way to finish came to her. "Maybe we *all* need ... a sanctuary."

The audience clapped enthusiastically.

"Well," said the Lord Mayor, rising from his chair, "judging by the audience reaction, there can be only one overall winner today. I give you: Jessica Brooke!"

More clapping. Some whooping. The Lord Mayor produced a gold statuette in the form of a large star and held it towards Molly.

The double doors at the end of the hall flew open and three people entered: a man, a woman and a girl around Molly's age.

"So sorry we're late!" said the woman.

"Who – who are you?" asked Liza Dreiser.

"Jessica Brooke, of course!" said the girl, in a voice as posh as her frock.

"Better give the trophy to her then," Molly said to the mayor, and exited stage left.

There was confusion in the hall. The audience were all talking loudly, Liza Dreiser was trying to take the award back from Jessica, and Jessica's parents were complaining to the mayor.

Molly heard the noise fade away behind her as she found a door that led back out to the Civic Centre. This was the *right* door, she decided.

Chapter 5

"Oh, *there* you are! Thank goodness!"

Gloria was standing by the fountain with Rani, Blake and Shirelle.

"We've been looking everywhere, for you!" said Shirelle.

"Well," said Molly, "I kept going through the wrong door."

She told her story and soon they were all laughing their heads off. And, when they were back in the Holiday Club, Gloria asked her to tell the story again and the whole group laughed. They were laughing *with* her, not *at* her, Molly knew.

"Did you have a good day, darling?" her mother asked,
when she came to pick Molly up at four o'clock.

"She's had quite a day!" said Gloria.

"How come?" asked Molly's mum, smiling.

"Tell you all about it in the car, Mum!"

"Looks like you've made friends with lots of people today," said Molly's mother as they walked back to the car park.

"Yeah," said Molly. "And I've *been* lots of different people too!"

It was a strange thing, Molly thought. You could decide for yourself what you'd be like at any time. She felt as if she had discovered something very important; something that gave her a new sense of freedom.

Four doors

🐾 Ideas for reading 🐾

Written by Clare Dowdall, PhD
Lecturer and Primary Literacy Consultant

Reading objectives:
- discuss the sequence of events in books and how items of information are related
- discuss and clarify the meanings of words, linking new meanings to known vocabulary
- make inferences on the basis of what is being said and done
- predict what might happen on the basis of what has been read so far

Spoken language objectives:
- use spoken language to develop understanding through speculating, hypothesising, imagining and exploring ideas
- participate in discussions, presentations, performances and debates

Curriculum links: PSHE – health and wellbeing; Writing – composition

Word count: 2500

Interest words: wander, retrace, miscalculation, self-admiring, remarkable, incomprehensible, emboldened, sanctuary

Resources: paper and pencils, dictionaries

Build a context for reading

- Look at the front cover and read the title *The Wrong Door*. Ask children if they have ever opened the wrong door somewhere by mistake – and to explain to the group what was behind it!
- Discuss where Molly is and what might have happened to her. Discuss what a holiday club is and what usually happens there.
- Challenge children to imagine how Molly might be feeling and develop their descriptive vocabulary, e.g. *she might be feeling desperate; anxious ...*
- Read the blurb with the children. Check that they understand what a "wander" is. Ask them to predict what Molly will find behind each door.

Understand and apply reading strategies

- Read Chapter 1 aloud to the children. As you read, ask them to think about how they would feel if they were in Molly's position.